The Great

CLOWN CONUNDRUM

The Big-Top
MYSTERIES

The Great
CLOWN
CONUNDRUM

ALEXANDER McCALL SMITH

With illustrations by Sam Usher

onkers

Conkers

First published in 2019 in Great Britain by
Barrington Stoke Ltd
18 Walker Street, Edinburgh, EH3 7LP

www.barringtonstoke.co.uk

Text © 2019 Alexander McCall Smith
Illustrations © 2019 Sam Usher

A CIP catalogue record for this book is available
from the British Library upon request

ISBN: 978-1-78112-880-0

Printed and bound in Great Britain by CPI Group (UK) Ltd, Croydon, CR0 4YY

Contents

CHAPTER 1

Getting ready for the show

Billy, Fern and Joe Shortbread were three children who lived in a circus owned by their parents, Henry and Doris Shortbread. You will not be surprised to hear that the circus was called Shortbreads' Great, Amazing and Wonderful Circus. It was one of the most popular circuses in the country, and people loved going to see it.

The Shortbread children all worked in the circus, but they did something else as well, which was even more remarkable than their circus jobs. All three of them had a special talent for detection. They were part-time detectives and solvers of mysteries, and they were rather good at that. Recently, for example, they had helped a boy find his granny after she had disappeared. That was just the sort of thing they liked to do – to help other people by skilfully investigating clues. It was exciting work, and they hoped to do more of it.

"There's nothing better than finding a clue and then solving it," said Billy, who was the eldest of the three.

"I agree," said his sister Fern.

"And so do I," said Joe, who was the youngest.

"And isn't it amazing how clues turn up once you start looking for them?"

Of course, the Shortbread children had to spend a lot of their time practising their circus acts. If you work in a circus, you have to make sure that you are really good at your act. If you are a juggler, for example, you can't allow yourself to drop any of the balls. Or if you are a trapeze artist, you have to have perfect timing or you might end up falling into the safety net below. You have to practise and then practise again, until everything goes like clockwork.

There were holidays, and you did not need to practise then, but when you came back from your holiday you had to spend a lot of time working on a new routine. Circus acts have to change, as the people who come to the show always want to see something fresh.

That year, at the end of their family holiday, the Shortbread children had three weeks to practise their new acts before the start of the new season. During these three weeks the circus was closed, so that rehearsals could take place without an audience. It was also a time when everybody lent a hand in carrying out repairs that had to be done to the circus equipment. The tent might have a small tear here and there that would have to be sewn up. The seats might need to be adjusted and made more stable. And the costumes that everybody wore might need to have glittering sequins replaced. There was always so much to do during the rehearsal period.

Billy was part of a bigger act called "Ruffy Ruffino and His High Fliers". This was run by Mr Ruffino, who was one of the country's most skilled and admired trapeze artists. He could swing backwards and forwards at a great height, sailing over the heads of the audience while holding on to the trapeze with only one hand. Sometimes he turned himself upside down and held on with his feet – which made everybody down below gasp with fear.

Billy was not quite as good as that, but he was certainly making good progress.

"You're getting better and better, Billy," Mr Ruffino said one day. "I think you might be able to try a blindfold act this season."

Billy realised how much of a compliment that was. "Do you think so?" he asked, trying not to sound too eager.

"Yes," said Mr Ruffino. "I think the time has come to start practising blindfold, Billy."

Billy was thrilled by this news, even if his heart was in his mouth when he first started swinging up on high with a thick black cloth tied over his eyes. And when Mr Ruffino told him to let go of the trapeze and sail through the air to catch a swing coming towards him, Billy was almost too frightened to do what he was told. But circus

people know that they have to trust the person training them, and so Billy did as he was asked. Fortunately it worked well, and he grabbed the other swing and shot up in a perfect arc towards the top of the tent.

There was a safety net, of course, and there were several occasions when Billy fumbled with a trapeze, or just missed it and plummeted down towards the net below.

Then he would bounce back up before falling back down again – and so it would continue until there was no more bounce left. But Billy became more and more expert in the new act, and by the time three weeks was up, he was a very polished performer – a credit, Mr Ruffino said, to "Ruffy Ruffino and His High Fliers".

Fern had a new acrobatic routine to practise for her act, "The Elastic Bouncing Girl". She had a fresh outfit to go with this – a bright red leotard on which there were sewn several white pom-poms. Dressed this way, Fern would then twist and tumble in the most amazing display of rubbery contortions you could imagine.

"That girl," said one of the ticket sellers, "can turn herself inside out – or almost."

Fern's routine for the new season used a

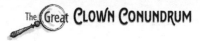

see-saw that shot her high in the air. This is how it worked: she would stand on the lowered end of the see-saw. At the other end – about three metres above the plank – stood a man on a ladder. When the man jumped off his ladder onto

the end of the see-saw, this would make the other end rise sharply. That shot Fern up into the air, where she turned several somersaults before landing neatly on her feet.

Billy and Joe had both seen her practise this new routine and thought it very good.

"I could never do that," Joe sighed.

"But Fern could never train dogs as well as you do," Billy said. "Each of us has special things we do. Each is as important as the other."

Joe was proud of the new trick he had dreamed up for his act, "Young Joe Shortbread and His Clever Dogs". For this, his dogs were all dressed in red fire-fighter outfits and helped to rescue toy cats trapped in a small model of a house. One of the dogs went down through the chimney, while another struggled to squeeze

through a window. Yet another pretended to drive a toy fire engine.

"That's very funny," said Fern, after she had watched a rehearsal. "But I'm not sure if real cats would ever let dogs rescue them. You know how cats can be."

"And I'm not sure if real dogs would want to rescue cats," Billy added with a smile.

Their father, though, was very pleased. "That doesn't matter," he said. "People go to the circus to laugh and have fun."

The important thing, Mr Shortbread said, was for the audience to enjoy themselves and forget, even if only for a little while, about the outside world and its problems. Inside the circus it would always feel the same, no matter what was happening outside. The circus was a world

in which the sun always shone, a place in which anything was possible. And a circus act would always work well if the person doing it practised hard enough.

"I'm proud of you," Doris Shortbread said to her children. "You're true circus people – and that's the best thing I can think to say about anybody!"

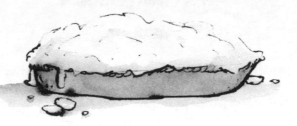

CHAPTER 2

A disaster occurs

At last, the opening day of the new season arrived.

"This is going to be one of the best shows ever," said Henry Shortbread on the morning of the opening. "Is everybody ready?"

There were nods from all the children.

"The dogs are really looking forward to it," said Joe. "I can tell they're excited."

"I'm looking forward to it too," said Fern. "I've practised and practised as hard as I possibly can."

"And I could hardly sleep last night," Billy said. "I kept thinking of my new blindfold act. I can't wait."

The other circus performers all said much the same thing. George Muscle, the circus strongman, who already drew gasps of admiration from audiences while he bent a thick iron bar with his bare hands, said that he was feeling even stronger than usual. Polly Fingerworth, the juggler, was also pleased with the improvements she'd made to her act.

"I can now keep seven balls in the air at the same time," she said. "And for the last week in rehearsals I haven't dropped a single one."

The circus clown, Mr Birdcage, was excited about the new part of his act that he had planned with his assistant, Paddy Broadfoot.

"I have a bigger than ever custard pie," he said. "And when I throw it at Paddy, it goes all over the place. You should see it! It's amazing. The crowd will love it."

Let me tell you a little bit about Mr Birdcage. Ronald Pomponius Birdcage – to give him his full name – had worked in the Shortbread Circus for as long as anybody could remember. He was the children's teacher, as they could not go to regular school, and so they knew him well – and liked him too. He made learning fun, as one might expect of a teacher who is also a circus clown. He was a tall man who walked in a rather gangly manner. And if you are wondering what gangly means, it is a word you can use to describe somebody whose arms and legs seem a bit floppy. They are all over the place – loose and floppy, like the limbs of a rag doll.

"I think that Mr Birdcage's legs aren't connected to his body in the same way as everybody else's," Fern once said. "It's very odd."

Billy agreed. "That's why he's so funny," he said. "People love his funny walk."

"And the way his face looks," Joe said. "The dogs all bark when he looks at them as he comes out of the ring."

Mr Birdcage did not mind any of this. He could walk in exactly the same way as everybody else, and when he wasn't performing, his face was not particularly funny. He looked funny

19

during his act because he deliberately walked in his gangly way and because he wore a large red plastic nose and a set of sticking-out false teeth. He made the circus audience laugh so much that some of them even cried!

They also found his clothes very amusing. None of the clothes that the clown wore seemed to fit him. He had a large jacket with blue spots that was big enough, people said, for at least two

men to fit inside it. That was funny enough, but then there were his shoes. These were at least twice the size of normal shoes, and they flipped and flapped on the ground with every step that he took. The crowd loved that.

Like everybody else who worked in the circus, Mr Birdcage lived in a caravan. But his caravan was different. When you opened the door to visit him, a hooter sounded from somewhere and a rubber bucket, half full of water, fell on your head. When you sat down inside, the cushion underneath you made a strange sound and the chair legs fell off. And when he gave you a cup of coffee, your lips would stick to the cup and the coffee itself would turn out to be treacle. It was all very funny.

Nobody, not even Henry and Doris Shortbread, knew where Mr Birdcage came from. From the very first day they had taken over the circus, he had been there, and he had never said much about his past, other than to tell them that he had once been a teacher. Nor did he appear to have any close family, although he had spoken now and then about having a brother.

"I have a brother called Sid," he once told Billy. "I haven't seen him for a while and he never writes any letters. But one of these days I'll go and see him again."

"What does he do?" asked Billy. He had tried to imagine what Sid Birdcage looked like. Billy thought that Sid, too, would have a funny walk and legs and arms that went all over the place.

Mr Birdcage did not seem to want to answer the question but shrugged as if to say that he really had no idea.

Mr Birdcage was very kind. If you were ever feeling a bit low, he would go out of his way to cheer you up. He would show you a flower that, when you tried to sniff it, shot a jet of water into your face. People loved that. Or he would reach out to shake your hand and a buzzer would tickle your palm. That was another good joke that would make you smile, no matter how miserable you might have been. And he always had a kind word for everybody. That would make people feel better, as saying a kind word to somebody never fails to make them feel better.

Paddy Broadfoot, his assistant, was not as

tall as Mr Birdcage, and although people smiled when they saw him, they did not laugh quite as much as they laughed at the older clown.

Paddy's job was to fall over whenever Mr Birdcage gave him a push. Then, when he got up, he had to trip over his own feet and end up on the ground once more. He also had to pretend not to notice when Mr Birdcage crept up behind him with a bucket of red paint and poured it over his head. For the crowd, that was the highlight of the whole show, and they laughed and laughed.

The two clowns were very popular – people loved their act. Many of the audience said that this was why they came to the circus – to see the clowns.

"Our circus would never be the same without Mr Birdcage," Henry Shortbread once said. "A circus without a clown is like a day without sunshine."

"Or a birthday without a cake," said Doris.

"Or a dog without a tail," Fern suggested.

"It's like all of those things," said her father.

"That's why Mr Birdcage is one of the most important people in our circus."

"He's the funniest clown in the country," said Billy.

"In the world," said Joe.

Mr Shortbread smiled. "Perhaps," he said, and then smiled again.

The first show of the new season was sold out. Every single seat was taken, and there were even people standing at the back. And as always before a show, there was an excited hum in the air.

George Muscle was the first to go on. He lifted several heavy weights with his little finger, causing gasps of surprise and admiration from the crowd. Then he invited four members of the

audience to come on stage and sit down on a
sofa. Crouching down, he lifted the sofa high up
in the air, along with everybody seated on it. The
applause was deafening.

After George Muscle came
the human cannonball –
always a popular act.
This involved a thin
man known as Albert
Longshot squeezing
himself into the mouth

of a large cannon. Once he had
disappeared down the muzzle, his wife, Mina,
struck a match and lit a fuse. People held their
breath as they watched the fuse burn down.
Then, with a puff of smoke and a loud bang,
Albert Longshot was shot out of the mouth of the
cannon to land in a net on the other side of the
tent. People screamed and clapped their hands at
that act, hardly believing such a thing possible.
But it was – for there was Albert, none the worse

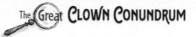
for his experience, jumping out of the safety net

and holding his arms up in the air in a gesture of

triumph.

Like all the others, Albert had now added

something new to his act. In his case, it was to

change the colour of the smoke that came out

of the cannon when it was fired. That used to be

white – just like ordinary smoke – but now it was

red and changed to orange after it had hung in

the air for a few moments. The crowd liked that

very much.

Next came Joe with his dogs. They were

always popular, and his new act went down very

well with the crowd. As did Billy's blindfolded

swinging with the Ruffinos. That was rather

frightening for some members of the audience,

who closed their eyes when they saw Billy

launched out into the air and only opened them again when he had safely caught the empty trapeze that had been swung towards him.

Fern's new acrobatic routine was a big hit too. Excited by the fact that she was putting on a new act, she performed especially well and was rewarded with a long burst of applause at the end. Watching her from the wings, Henry and Doris Shortbread gave each other a proud glance, pleased that Fern, as well as Billy and Joe, had put on such a good performance on this first night of the new season.

Now it was the turn of Mr Birdcage and Paddy Broadfoot.

In they came, falling over each other and thumping one another on the back in time to a roll of drums. They were greeted with gales of

laughter, everybody leaning forwards in their seats to make sure they did not miss any of the fun.

After a few minutes of running around and falling over, it was time for the new highlight of the act – the custard-pie throwing. There were plenty of chuckles from all corners of the tent when Mr Birdcage took an extremely large custard pie out of a box and prepared to throw it at Paddy Broadfoot.

He practised the throw for some time, while Paddy pretended not to see what was going on.

"Be careful!" shouted a boy from the back of the tent.

Paddy Broadfoot just grinned, still pretending not to be aware of the danger he was in of being covered in custard pie.

"Look behind you!" shouted a girl from the

front row. But Paddy just grinned again and scratched his head. And then Mr Birdcage lifted the pie into the air, whirled it round and round and sent it spinning towards his assistant, just like a giant frisbee.

His aim was good. The custard pie flew through the air and landed right on top of Paddy's head, just as Mr Birdcage had intended. But then something very odd happened. Normally, when a custard pie lands on your head, the custard falls out of the pie in a great deluge of yellow. It then covers your face, drips off your chin and spreads in a sticky tide all over you. That is what usually happens, but in this case, despite the huge size of the new pie, not one drop of custard dripped out of it. Instead, the pie simply bounced off the other clown's head, to land, with a thud, at his feet.

This was very disappointing for the crowd. They had wanted to see somebody covered in sticky custard. They did not expect to see what they saw. Nor did Mr Birdcage, who stared in

astonishment at this unexpected turn of events. Nor was he prepared for the silence that followed. Nobody clapped. Nobody laughed. Nobody knew what to do.

After this disappointment, the clowns' act quickly came to an end. There were one or two other tumbles and trippings-up, but the crowd didn't think these were very funny. At last, when Mr Birdcage and Paddy took their bow and disappeared from the ring, there were a few seconds of half-hearted applause and then nothing. The act had been a failure.

The three Shortbread children had watched in complete astonishment.

"Nothing like this has ever happened before," whispered Fern.

"It's a disaster," replied Billy.

"What happened?" asked Joe. "What went wrong?"

Neither Billy nor Fern knew how to answer their younger brother, but it was clear to them that something had gone very wrong indeed, and they wanted to find out what that was.

"Poor Mr Birdcage," Fern said. "He'll be so upset. He's always been laughed at, and now ... well, it's not easy when the crowd suddenly stop laughing, is it?"

CHAPTER 3

More things go wrong

The following morning, after breakfast, Billy
and Fern called round to Mr Birdcage's caravan
while Joe was feeding his performing dogs. They
found the famous clown sitting on the steps,
deep in thought. He looked up when he saw them,
and he tried to smile but clearly found it a bit
difficult.

"We thought we'd check that you're all right," said Fern. "After last night ..."

She did not finish what she was saying, as her words seemed to bring a look of distress to Mr Birdcage's face.

"Last night," he muttered. "Last night was a disaster – the worst performance ever in the history of clowning."

"Oh, don't say that," Billy urged. "I heard a lot of people laughing."

Mr Birdcage shook his head sadly. "They were laughing out of embarrassment. It was that sort of laughter, you see – the sort of laughter we laugh when something unfortunate happens to somebody else. Nervous laughter – that's what it was."

Billy could not argue with that. Mr Birdcage was right: it had been a disaster. He wondered, though, what had happened to the custard pie. Had it been over-cooked? Was that the trouble?

He asked Mr Birdcage what he thought had gone wrong.

"As you saw," said Mr Birdcage, "the pie

didn't work. It should have splashed drippy custard all over Paddy. It didn't. The custard had turned as hard as rock."

Fern was puzzled. "Was it like that at the beginning of the act?" she asked.

"No," said Mr Birdcage. "When I took it into the tent, it was all gooey, just as it should be. It changed during the time that Paddy and I were falling about."

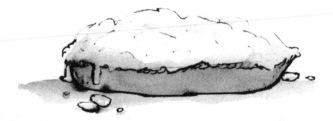

Billy looked thoughtful. "So it must have had something in it that made it go stiff," he said.

"Yes," said Mr Birdcage. "But the curious thing is that I followed my usual recipe to the letter. I used exactly the same ingredients. The only change was that I used larger amounts."

"And that should have had no effect on how soft it was," Fern observed. She had seen Mr Birdcage practising the mixing of his pies time and time again, and she knew that if something had gone wrong, it could not be his fault.

"You're right," said Mr Birdcage. "It should have been exactly the same." He sighed deeply. "But it wasn't."

"That's very mysterious," said Billy. "Do you think that somebody did something to it? Do you think that somebody added something to your ingredients?"

As successful detectives, Billy and Fern had

learned to be on the lookout for anything suspicious. If something odd was happening, then that was the time to look for clues as to why this should be so. It was as if an alarm bell was going off.

Mr Birdcage looked doubtful. "I keep my supplies of custard powder in the same place as all my other bits and pieces – in my storage caravan next door. And the door of that is always kept locked when I'm not using it."

"Could you show us the storage caravan?" asked Billy.

Mr Birdcage rose to his feet. "There won't be much to see," he said. "But if you think it'll help, I'll open it up for you."

They all made their way to the caravan

where Mr Birdcage kept the props he needed for his act. The door was locked, as he said it would be, and Billy noted that there was no sign of it

having been forced open. Once inside, they could see all the things that clowns need – greasepaint for the face, floppy hats in bright colours, bendy walking sticks and, of course, any number of red plastic noses. There were also several large

packets of yellow powder for the large custard
pies that were to be the new highlight of the act.

Billy examined these packets carefully. At
first he saw nothing unusual
about them, but then, as
he peered more closely, he
noticed that there was a tiny
hole in one packet. It was
not an ordinary hole – the
sort of hole that might come from
a weakness in the packaging; this hole looked as
if it might have been deliberately made – perhaps
with a knife. He pointed this out to Mr Birdcage.

"That hole, Mr Birdcage – was it always
there?"

Mr Birdcage frowned. "I'm not sure, Billy.
Perhaps it was, but then again perhaps it was not."

"I wonder if somebody could have put something into the packet," said Billy. "Some chemical that would make the custard go hard."

Fern had noticed something else. She had seen that some of the custard powder had trickled down out of the hole and was now on the floor. And more than that, somebody had stepped in the spilled powder and left a couple of yellow footprints going off towards the door. "I think that somebody came in here and deliberately put something into your custard powder," she said. "And there are the footprints to prove it."

Mr Birdcage was silent. Then he said, "But why? Who would try to ruin my act?"

Billy could not answer that, and nor could Fern.

"I don't think I've got any enemies," Mr Birdcage continued. "I haven't done anything nasty to anybody."

Billy was quick to agree. "Of course you haven't," he said. Mr Birdcage was one of the kindest men he knew, and the idea that the clown would have an enemy seemed ridiculous.

They suggested to Mr Birdcage that he should get rid of the suspect packet of custard powder. "Use another packet tonight," they said. "And be careful to keep the door of the caravan locked."

The clown agreed that this would be a wise precaution and, with that, Billy and Fern said goodbye and went back to their own family caravan.

"I do hope that everything goes smoothly tonight," said Fern. "It would be awful if Mr Birdcage were to have another disaster."

"He won't," said Billy. "I'm sure it will all be fine."

But even as he spoke, he realised that he was in fact far from sure. Billy felt certain that there was a mystery

here – and a worrying one – and so far they had discovered only one clue: the footprints on the floor. And that clue, unfortunately, did not tell them very much.

At that night's performance, Mr Shortbread had arranged for the clowns to come on last. He sometimes did this so that people left the circus with a smile on their faces – always a good way to end an evening. So by the time that Mr Birdcage and Paddy Broadfoot came on, the crowd was well warmed up and ready for some boisterous fun.

It all went well to begin with. The clowns stumbled and fell and hit each other over the head with rubber hammers. The trick with the bucket of red paint went down very well and they

were just about to
start on the custard
pies when something
strange happened. Mr Birdcage suddenly stopped
in his tracks and began to scratch under his coat
as if he had a very annoying itch. A few moments
later, Paddy Broadfoot started to do exactly the
same.

Billy looked at Fern, who shrugged and
looked at Joe. Was this planned? Was this a new
part of the clowns' act?

It was not. Mr Birdcage and Paddy Broadfoot
were now looking very uncomfortable, and their
itching seemed to have become much worse.
Eventually, they had to bow and run out of the
ring before the custard pie was thrown, much to
the puzzlement and disappointment of the crowd.

Some people actually booed, thinking that all the
scratching was a rather weak joke and not at all
funny. They did not know, of course, that this was
not part of the act, but that the two clowns really

were itching – they were itching so badly that they needed to get back to their caravans as soon as they possibly could and have a shower.

And it was only the shower that stopped the itching, as it always will when somebody has put itching powder in your clothes.

CHAPTER 4

Keeping watch in the dark

"Itching powder!" exclaimed Fern after the show.

"Yes," said Billy. "Mr Birdcage said that is what happened. Somebody had put itching powder in his jacket – and in Paddy's as well."

Joe was intrigued. He had never heard of itching powder before. "How does this itching powder work?" he asked.

"It's not a very nice thing," Billy explained. "It irritates the skin and you have to scratch. Some people think it's funny, but I don't. It doesn't really harm you, but it's not a nice feeling."

Fern was thinking. "This must be the same person who sabotaged Mr Birdcage's act last night," she said. "Now they've struck again."

"Yes," said Billy. "And what a nasty, low thing to do."

Fern looked worried. "Do you know where Mr Birdcage keeps his clown outfits?" she asked.

Billy thought that it was in the same caravan where he kept his other props, including the custard powder.

"Somebody must be getting in there somehow," said Fern.

"But the door is always locked," Billy pointed

out. "Mr Birdcage told us that."

"Then they're getting in another way," Fern argued. "Or they have a key – who knows?"

"It must be happening at night," said Billy. "Otherwise somebody would see them."

Billy thought about this. He was worried about what was happening. Not only did it make him sad to see poor Mr Birdcage's act ruined, but he was concerned, too, about what this meant for the circus. If word got out that Shortbreads' Circus had an unfunny clown, whose act was always going wrong, then people would either go to another circus – one with clowns who made them laugh – or not go to a circus at all. Either way, that would mean that their parents' circus would make less money, and if it did not make enough money, then how would people be paid? And if people weren't paid, they would go and work somewhere else, and that would be the end of the circus.

Of course, that hardly bore thinking about. If Mr and Mrs Shortbread had to close the circus, then where would the family live? In a house? That would not be too bad, Billy thought – lots of people lived in houses and seemed quite happy about it. But living in a caravan was far greater fun, he thought. If you lived in a caravan, you had a different view each time you moved. If you lived in a caravan, you could sometimes wake up in the morning and see the countryside all about you, with cows and sheep and birds in the trees, and a river, perhaps, with fish swimming in its pools. And in the summer you could swim in the river,

and splash and throw stones that skimmed across the surface of the water ... Oh, there were so many things that made it fun to live in a caravan.

For a few minutes, Billy was lost in his thoughts and did not hear what Fern said. But then she repeated her question to him. "What are we going to do, Billy? We can't do nothing."

"No," Billy replied. "We can't do nothing." He paused. "Nothing is definitely what we can't do."

"Which means that we must do something," Fern said.

Billy's mind was made up. The idea had come to him very suddenly, and he had not thought it out, but it seemed a rather good idea to him, and now he revealed it to his sister.

"We are going to watch the caravan where he keeps things," he said. "We're going to find somewhere to hide tonight, and we're going to

see if anybody tries to get in to sabotage Mr Birdcage's act again for tomorrow."

Fern's eyes widened. "Just us?" she said.

"Yes," Billy replied. "And Joe too."

"Will Mum and Dad let us?" asked Fern. She

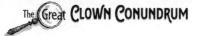

was worried that their parents would insist that they went to bed as normal.

"I'll ask," said Billy. "We won't be far away from our own caravan – just around the corner. I'm sure they'll agree."

And they did. When Billy went to speak to his parents, he found Mr and Mrs Shortbread sitting at the caravan table looking extremely worried.

Mr Birdcage had been to see them, they explained, and he had told them that Paddy Broadfoot was going to leave the circus. He had been thinking of going to live in Australia, where he had been offered a job as chief clown in a circus, and all the problems they'd been having with the act had simply made up his mind for him.

"This makes matters even worse for Mr

Birdcage," Mr Shortbread said. "A clown needs an assistant. He needs somebody to throw custard pies at and fall over with. What will happen when Paddy goes?"

Billy had no answer to that, and so when he told his parents about his plan to try to catch the

person who was sabotaging the clowns' act, they readily agreed.

"Don't do anything dangerous," Henry Shortbread said. "Be very careful."

Billy nodded. "We always are," he assured his father. "Good detectives are always careful."

"Good," said his father. "Good luck, then."

"I'm very proud that my children are detectives," Doris Shortbread said to her husband after Billy had gone off. "How many parents can say, 'Our children are famous detectives'? Very few, I think."

"And they're nice people too," Mr Shortbread mused. "Each one of them is a nice person."

"Amazing," said Mrs Shortbread.

Billy and Fern found a good place to hide, which was in an empty wooden crate used to transport poles for the Big Top. The crate was lying on its side, and if they hid in it they would be able to look through the slats of wood and see what was happening outside. In particular, they had a good view of the caravan they wanted to keep an eye on.

Billy looked at his watch. It was already quite late, and the last of the evening light had faded from the sky. He and Fern had explained the plan to Joe, and he now joined them, after feeding his dogs, excited to be involved in an important investigation.

"What if we see somebody?" Joe asked. "What then?"

"If we do," Billy said, "Fern will run off to tell Dad. He'll come and deal with the intruder."

Fern shivered. "I'm a bit scared," she said.

Billy hesitated. "Well, I'm a bit scared too," he admitted.

"And me too," said Joe.

"So we'll all run off and get help," Billy decided.

"That's a good idea," said Fern.

Because it was so late, Fern suggested that they take it in turns to stay awake and keep watch. That would mean that while one person was watching, the other two would be able to doze off until it was time for one of them to take over. Billy and Joe agreed that this was the best thing to do, and Joe immediately volunteered to be the first on duty.

For a long time, nothing happened. The night dragged on, as nights always seem to do, and it was not until well into the early hours of the morning, when dawn was still some hours off, that something happened.

There was a full moon that night, bathing
the circus and all about it with a gentle silvery
light. There were patches of dark, however,
and some of these seemed to move. That was
the breeze, of course, which played amongst
the branches of trees, sending shadows across
the ground. If there had been only one of them
keeping watch through the night, that person
would have been very scared indeed. But with
three of them, even if two were asleep, it did not
feel quite so lonely or scary.

Then it happened. Fern was on watch at the
time, and she saw a shadow move. At first, she
thought it might just be a shadow from one of the
trees, but then it moved again, and she saw that
it had the shape of a person. For a few moments,
her heart beat furiously with fright.

"Billy," she whispered, nudging her drowsy brother. "Billy, there's somebody coming."

Billy struggled up out of sleep. He had been dreaming, and when he woke up he forgot where he was. But then he remembered, and he gently shook Joe to wake him up too. Then, peering through a space between two slats of wood, he saw the shape that had alerted Fern. Just as she had said, it was a person.

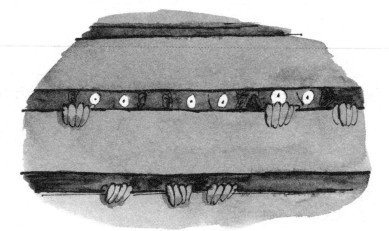

They watched as the figure approached the storage caravan. They saw him creep past the door and make his way to a window at the side.

They watched as he fished for something from his pocket and began to force open the window. *So that was how he had managed to get into the caravan,* Billy said to himself. *We should have thought of that.*

Fern nudged Billy. "I think we should run off to get help," she whispered.

Billy nodded. "Are you ready, Joe?" he asked, his voice lowered as far as he could.

Joe was already on his feet. "Let's go," he said, his voice wavering and barely audible. *How I wish my dogs were with me,* he thought. *They would always look after us.*

The three brave detectives crept out of their hiding place and began to make their way back to their own caravan, where they planned to wake their parents. Unfortunately, because of

the darkness, Joe tripped over an untied shoelace.
Down he went and, as he did so, he let out an
involuntary cry.

Billy spun round. He saw the figure about to
clamber up into the forced window. He saw him
stop and turn around when he heard Joe's cry.

"Oh no!" Billy muttered. "He's seen us."

CHAPTER 5

A good clue at last

When he noticed the three children creeping out of their hiding place, the man in the shadows stood quite still. Then, abandoning his attempt to climb in the window of the caravan, he turned and ran away, disappearing into the same darkness from which he had emerged.

"Stop!" shouted Billy at the top of his lungs.

"We saw you!" shouted Fern, waving her arms.

"So did I!" yelled Joe, feeling much braver because of the shouting.

It made no difference. The furtive figure had gone, and when Mr Shortbread, woken up by the noise, appeared in his dressing gown, there was no sign of him.

Others came to find out what all the fuss was about. Albert Longshot, the human cannonball, appeared in a pair of flaming red pyjamas, and he was followed by others, including the strongman, George Muscle.

Fern explained what had happened. Mr Shortbread and the others listened carefully, and they all then went to examine the caravan to see if any damage had been done. They could see where a screwdriver had been pushed into the side of the window, but apart from a scratch or two on the paintwork there was no other sign of the attempted break-in.

It was Joe who saw something, bending down to pick up what looked like a piece of paper. "What's this?" he said.

Billy shone his torch on the paper. "It's an envelope," he said. "Somebody must have dropped it."

Mr Shortbread did not seem interested. "People are always dropping litter," he said. "We ask them not to, but they do." He looked at his watch. "It's very late. I think we should all go to bed."

Albert Longshot congratulated the children on chasing away the intruder. "That's that," he said. "We've probably seen the last of him for a little while."

"Yes," agreed Mr Shortbread. "I don't think there'll be any more attempts to wreck Mr Birdcage's act. You three have scared off the intruder and solved the mystery, so to speak. Well done!"

Billy was not so sure. As they made their way back to their caravan with their father, he asked Joe for the envelope he had picked up.

Joe had put this away in his pocket, and now he fished it out and handed it to his brother.

"We'll examine it tomorrow," Billy whispered to Fern. "I think we may have found a clue."

They had. After breakfast the next morning Billy, Fern and Joe met outside the kennel where Joe kept his dogs. Billy took the envelope from his pocket and smoothed out the creases.

"We have to decide something," he said to the others.

They waited.

"We have to decide," he went on, "whether we think this is just a piece of litter, dropped by somebody in the crowd, or whether it could have been dropped by that man who was trying to break into Mr Birdcage's storage caravan, whoever he was."

They waited again. Then Fern asked, "How can we tell?"

"We can't," said Billy. "But let's say it *is* a clue. After all, people from the audience aren't allowed back among the caravans, and we did find it right under the window the intruder was trying to force."

"All right," said Fern. "It's a clue. What next?"

"We go to the address written on the envelope," said Billy. "Look, here it is."

He showed her the envelope. There was no letter inside it, but on the outside somebody had written an address. The name was smudged, but they could still make out a number, a street and a town.

Fern examined the envelope. "It's this town," she said. "It's right here."

"Yes," said Billy. "And we could easily find out where that street is. Albert Longshot had a map, he said. We could borrow it from him."

Joe was uneasy. "Why?" he asked. "What are we going to do? What if that is where the intruder lives? What then?"

"We could investigate," said Billy. He liked that word – *investigate*. That was what detectives did. They investigated clues, which was exactly what they were now doing.

"And then?" asked Joe.

"We'll see," said Billy. "You can never tell what's going to happen."

Fern asked Billy when they would start their investigation.

"Right now," said Billy. "We'll go and see what we can find."

Joe looked at Fern. He wondered whether she felt as scared as he did. She looked back at him and wondered whether *he* was as scared as *she* was.

Billy stood up, tucking the envelope back into his pocket. He was trying not to feel scared but was not succeeding very well. He hoped that

the other two would not notice – they looked so brave, he thought.

Using Albert Longshot's map, the three detectives rode their bicycles to the address on the envelope. It was not a long journey, and eventually they found themselves in the street named on the envelope. And then, a minute or two later, they were at the address itself.

Fern looked at Billy. "Is this it?" she asked.

Billy took the envelope out of his pocket and read it once again. "Yes," he said.

Joe pointed to the notice outside the building. "Sid's School of … " he started to read, but the paint had come off the last word and he could not make it out.

"It's a school," Billy said. "But the sign is so faded that I don't know what it's a school of."

Fern sighed. "Well, we can't just stand here," she said. "We need to go and take a look."

It was just the right suggestion to make, and Billy and Joe readily agreed. Parking their bicycles, they crept round the side of the building, trying to look into the windows as they did so. But most of the windows had been painted over, and they could not see through them. And it was all very quiet.

"Where are the students?" asked Joe. "What use is a school without students?"

"None," said Billy. "Perhaps they've all gone away because the school was no use."

Round the back of the building there was a large red door. This was half open, but it was too dark to see much inside.

"We could go in," whispered Billy.

Fern looked worried. "But what if somebody comes?" she said, her voice lowered.

"We'll be very quiet," Billy told her. "Nobody will hear us."

Joe was thinking of dogs. "What if there's a dog?" he asked. "Dogs can hear you even if people can't. And what if the dog starts to bark?"

"We'll be all right," Billy said, trying to sound as confident as he possibly could. *But will we?* he asked himself.

Billy led the way through a small entrance hall into a dusty room – a classroom of some sort, but one that had clearly not been used for some time. There were chairs and there was a blackboard. There were cupboards.

"Let's look in one of the cupboards," Fern

suggested. She had no idea what they might find

in the cupboard, but if you were looking around

somewhere and you found a cupboard, then she

thought that you should certainly look inside.

Billy agreed. Crossing the floor to one of the cupboards, he very slowly opened the door. It was a large walk-in cupboard, rather like a pantry, and it was lined with shelves. And on the shelves were ...

Joe heard a noise. "Somebody's coming," he hissed.

"We'll hide inside the cupboard," Billy said, pushing both Joe and Fern inside and closing the door behind him. Now they were in the dark – and it was a very dusty dark. Nobody had hidden in *this* cupboard for a very long time, thought Billy.

The cupboard door did not close properly, and a small chink was left open. It was by peering through this small gap that Billy was able to see the figure who had entered the classroom. The man had his back to Billy, but he could tell, from the figure's height and way of walking, that he could very well be the person they had seen in the shadows the night before.

And then the man turned round so that Billy could see his face, and the sight made him catch his breath. It was Mr Birdcage!

Billy turned to draw Fern's attention to what he had seen. But as he did so, he noticed something else. There was just enough light from the chink in the door to reveal what was on the shelves. Clown props. Pairs of outsize shoes. Red noses. Bendy walking sticks. All the things a clown might need – and lots of them.

CHAPTER 6

Everything is sorted out

The Shortbread children did not have to stay in the cupboard long. Mr Birdcage seemed to have come into the classroom only to collect a broom, and once he had that he went back the way he had come. This gave the children the chance to creep out of the building and run as fast as they could back to their bicycles.

Nothing was said on the way back to the circus. Nobody discussed it, but they had all decided the same thing: the only thing to do now was to tell their parents everything that had happened. Perhaps they would be able to throw some light on the mystery, because neither Billy nor Fern, or Joe either, could think of any explanation for what they had seen.

They sat round the kitchen table of their caravan and related the full story. At the end, Fern said, "It was Mr Birdcage we saw. We all saw him. It was definitely Mr Birdcage."

"But why would Mr Birdcage try to break into his own store?" Billy said. "And why would he want to sabotage his own act?"

Henry Shortbread shook his head. "I just don't believe it," he said. "Mr Birdcage wouldn't spoil his own show, would he, Doris?"

Mrs Shortbread agreed. "I think you must be mistaken," she said. "People sometimes look alike. And you said it was dark."

"Inside the cupboard," Fern corrected her. "It was dark *inside*. But in the classroom it was light. We saw him. We really did."

Henry Shortbread reached a decision. "I'm going to call Mr Birdcage in," he said. "We can ask him for an explanation."

He left the caravan and a few minutes later returned with Mr Birdcage. The clown smiled at everybody and joined them at the table.

"Now, Ronald," began Mr Shortbread, his voice still warm and friendly, "Billy and Fern and Joe have come up with some very curious information."

Mr Birdcage looked interested. "Oh? And what is that, may I ask?"

Henry Shortbread looked severe. "They found a clue when somebody tried to get into your storeroom last night."

"Really?" asked Mr Birdcage. "What kind of clue?"

"An envelope," said Mr Shortbread. "And this envelope led them to—"

"Sid's School," interjected Billy. "And we found a cupboard with clowns' things in it, and then—"

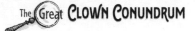
"And then we saw you," Fern finished up.

There was complete silence. Nobody spoke. Mr Birdcage's mouth opened as if he was about to speak, but then it closed again. He looked astounded.

"Was it you?" asked Mr Shortbread.

Mr Birdcage looked down at the floor. "Oh dear," he muttered, his voice barely loud enough to be heard. Then he added, "Oh dear, oh double dear!"

"Well?" Mrs Shortbread prompted. "How do you explain all that, Ronald?"

Mr Birdcage looked up. "Did I ever tell you I have a brother?" he said quietly.

Mr Shortbread looked thoughtful. "Well, yes, you did, I think."

"A twin," said Mr Birdcage. "He looks exactly like me. People can't tell us apart. And his name is Sid."

Again there was complete silence, broken eventually by Mrs Shortbread, who said, "So that explains it. But if the man the children saw was your

brother, and if it was the same person who tried to get into the caravan, then that means your twin brother was the person who was trying to ruin your act." She frowned. "Does that make sense?"

Mr Birdcage let out a very long sigh. It was a sigh filled with sadness.

"I'm afraid it does," he said. "My brother Sid, you see, has always been very envious of me. We both trained as clowns, but I was much more successful than he was. I was better than he was, I suppose, at just about everything. And he felt very bad about that."

The clown looked about him. Everybody felt sorry for him now. Everybody was listening very quietly.

"He started a clown school," continued Mr Birdcage. "He called it Sid's School of Clowning. But it was never very successful. He had a few people who came to learn how to be a clown but

not many. And all the time lots and lots of people were laughing at me here at Shortbreads' Great, Amazing and Wonderful Circus, but nobody ever laughed at him. I think that was too much for him to bear."

Mr Shortbread reached out to put a hand on Mr Birdcage's arm. "I'm so sorry to hear all this, Ronald. It's a very sad tale."

"Yes," said Mr Birdcage. "And now, I suppose, he must have decided to ruin my act because he couldn't stand the idea that I was doing so well and getting all those laughs."

"That sometimes happens," said Mrs Shortbread. "People can get so envious of the success of others that they just want to ruin it for them. They want attention. They want people to notice them, to like them, and they think – quite wrongly – that the way to do it is to do something unpleasant."

"I'm afraid that's true," said Mr Birdcage. "Poor Sid."

And that is when Fern had her idea. Later on, she would realise that this was one of the best ideas anybody has ever had, but at the time it seemed to her to be just an ordinary idea.

"Didn't you say that Paddy Broadfoot was going to be leaving?" she asked her parents.

"Yes," said Mrs Shortbread. "That's correct, isn't it, Ronald?"

Mr Birdcage nodded sadly. "He wants to go next week. He's going to work in a circus in Australia."

"Well then," said Fern. "Why don't you offer your brother Paddy's job?"

Mr Birdcage looked puzzled. "Here? With me?"

"Yes," said Fern. "If he's been so envious, then why don't you give him the chance to be very funny himself? Why not help him to be laughed at?"

Mrs Shortbread had been listening very carefully to Fern's suggestion. Now she smiled. "But, yes! Yes! That's what you should do with people who don't feel good about themselves. Build them up. Be kind to them. Tell them they're great. Let the light shine on them for a change. It often works, you know."

For a few moments, nobody spoke. Then Mr Birdcage started to nod. "You know what?" he said. "I think Fern has come up with the best idea I've heard for years. All this time I've been wondering

97

what to do for poor Sid, and now Fern has found the answer. It's just the right thing to do."

"Would you make him the joint star of your show?" asked Mr Shortbread.

"Yes," said Mr Birdcage. "We could call the act 'The Birdcage Brothers'."

"How about 'The Bumbling Birdcage Brothers'?" suggested Billy.

"Brilliant," said Mr Birdcage. But then he had a further thought and added, "Or 'Sid and Ronald Birdcage, Bumbling Brothers'. That would put Sid's name first. He'd love that. He'd no longer feel envious."

Mr Shortbread smiled broadly. He was sure they had found a solution – not only for the problem of what to do when Paddy Broadfoot left but also for the problem of Sid Birdcage's envy

of his brother. Often, he thought, the cure for
unhappiness is simply a bit of happiness – and
laughter, of course. Laughter was important too –
as strong as many medicines you could think of.

It was not hard for Mr Birdcage to persuade
his brother to join him. Two days later, they did

their first show together. Mr Birdcage went out
of his way to let Sid take the lead, and all the
jokes went very well indeed. There was a great

deal of applause for both of them, but if anybody was clapped slightly louder, then that was Sid. The crowd loved him. And as the applause rose, so loud that it filled the great tent with sound – and as the laughter rolled and rolled – Billy thought he could see Sid growing before their eyes. He seemed taller now; his smile grew wider; he fell about and tripped over his shoes with greater and greater style and confidence. And Mr Birdcage, who had missed his brother, and who had always hoped that they would be friends again one day, smiled with pleasure at what was happening.

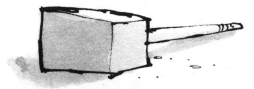

To celebrate the success of the clowns, the Shortbread family had a party. Everybody was invited, including Albert Longshot, the human

cannonball; Polly Fingerworth, the juggler; and George Muscle, the strongman. They all said how pleased they were that the two clowns were proving so popular and that the brothers were together again.

Mrs Shortbread made a special cake for the occasion with a great deal of icing and cream. It was very tempting for the clowns, because such a cake is just asking to be thrown, but I'm happy to say they did not do that. They very politely passed slices round to everybody, and it was enjoyed by all the guests. Joe, in particular, liked it so much that he asked for, and was given, an extra slice.

Mr Shortbread made a short speech. "Long speeches can be very boring," he said, "so I shall be brief."

"That's right, Henry," said Mrs Shortbread. "Don't speak for too long. People have cake to eat."

"All I'd like to say," said Mr Shortbread, "is

that we are very lucky in this circus. We have very fine performers. We have very, very funny clowns, and we have three extremely good detectives. We are lucky."

"And really nice dogs," Joe reminded his father, pointing to his dogs, who had been invited as well and who were busy sniffing out crumbs from the floor.

"And really nice dogs," echoed Mr Shortbread.

"I've forgotten something," Mrs Shortbread suddenly said. "I made a custard pie as well as a cake. Would anybody like some custard pie – to eat, that is, not to throw?"

They all laughed, and then they all said yes.

WHO DID IT?

Someone's knocked Mr Birdcage's custard pie onto the floor!

Billy, Fern and Joe have spotted footprints leading away from the mess. Can you help them work out which suspect's footprints lead back to the custard pie?

SUSPECT A

Did George Muscle knock it over with his iron bar?

SUSPECT B

Did Paddy Broadfoot trip over his big shoes?

SUSPECT C

Did Polly Fingerworth hit it with one of her balls?

Answer on page 112

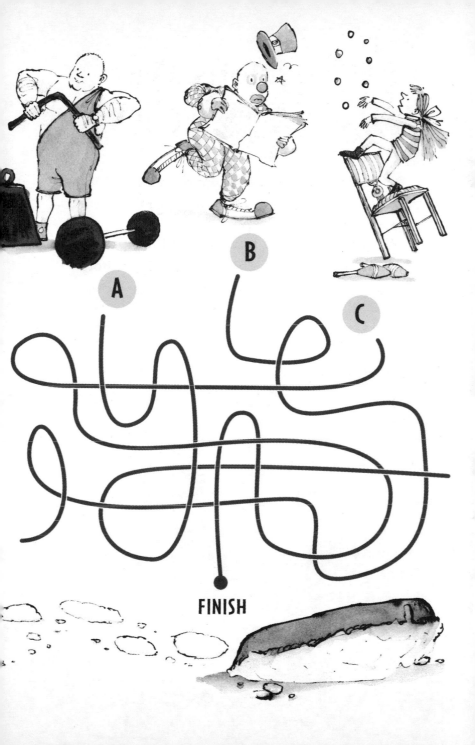

A

B

C

FINISH

CAN YOU BECOME A WORD DETECTIVE?

Detectives like Billy, Fern and Joe have to be good at tracking down hidden clues in all sorts of places. Can you put on your detective hat to find the words below?

acrobat ☐

trapeze ☐

strongman ☐

juggle ☐

cannon ☐

clown ☐

detective ☐

mystery ☐

clue ☐

footprints ☐

t	r	a	p	e	z	e	z	e
d	e	t	e	c	t	i	v	e
h	f	e	t	l	p	v	j	b
c	o	a	o	o	j	e	i	c
o	o	c	f	w	u	d	i	a
s	t	r	o	n	g	m	a	n
c	p	o	u	a	g	y	y	n
x	r	b	f	j	l	s	z	o
p	i	a	u	c	e	t	m	n
r	n	t	k	w	h	e	n	n
e	t	c	l	u	e	r	e	s
q	s	l	d	v	m	y	y	r

Answer on page 113

WHO DID IT?
ANSWER:
POLLY FINGERWORTH

A

B

C

FINISH

Can You Become A Word Detective?

ANSWERS:

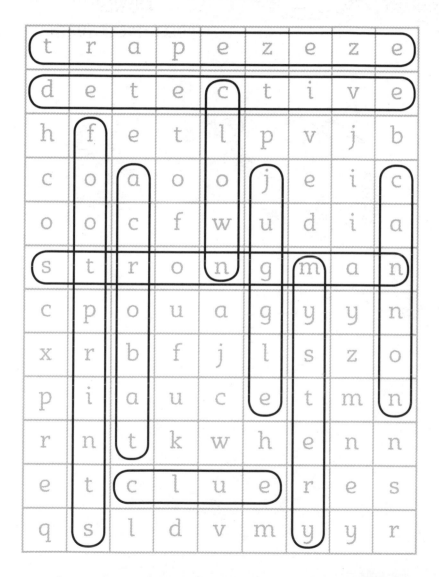